EXTREME MONSTERS™

THE BLUE MOON EFFECT

BY MEL FRIEDMAN

ILLUSTRATED BY ERIC SMITH

Extreme Monsters™ created
by Randy Meredith and Eric Smith

A Penny Candy Press™ Book

Brighter Minds Children's Publishing
Columbus • Toronto

Cover by Eric Smith

Library of Congress Control Number: 2005931101

ISBN 1-57791-178-4

www.pennycandypress.com

Printed in the United States of America

1 2 3 4 5   09 08 07 06 05

CONTENTS

CHAPTER ONE

Meltdown

Val gazed up the long hill at the Monsterey Valley Extreme Sports Park and cocked his head to one side. He was straining to identify a faint and troubling noise. The eleven-year-old captain of the Extreme Monsters sports team had always been a kid who was tuned in to his environment. He could walk into a friend's room and instantly tell if a book was out of place. But being half vampire as well as half human, he also possessed certain supernatural gifts. He could fly great distances in the blink of an eye. He could disguise himself as mist. And he had unbelievably powerful hearing. When he wanted to, he could detect the *plink!* of a dime dropped in a busy bowling alley.

At the present moment, Val's amazing ears were

focused on a lone figure about half a mile away. The girl was dressed in a full body suit and leather gloves. She was about to take a practice run down the winding street-luge course. It was clear from the disturbed look on Val's face that he didn't like what he was hearing.

"Something's up!" he called out to his companion, a shaggy-haired werewolf named Wulf. Val lifted the Strong-Site binoculars to his eyes to get a better view.

Wulf, the Extreme Monsters' in-line skating daredevil, hit a Berani—a front flip where the young werewolf landed facing in the opposite direction from the one he started. "What?" he said. Wulf glided over to the guardrail where Val was standing.

Val pointed toward the top of the hill, where their friend Jinx was sitting on her sleek new aluminum street luge, a racing sled on wheels. She'd rolled it into the track's paddle zone several minutes earlier. Now she was rocking it back and forth to get a feel for the wheel action. It was the sound of that motion that had caught Val's attention.

"What do you see?" asked Wulf.

"Nothing," said Val. "But Jinx's sled is making a weird noise."

"Like what?"

"It's too faint for human ears, but it sounds like...like..." Val paused and lowered the Strong-Sites, looking a little embarrassed.

"Like what?" the werewolf persisted.

"Like sizzling bacon. You know, tiny crackles and pops?"

"Dude, you are kidding!" laughed Wulf. "Are you sure you didn't get your signals scrambled? Maybe you're picking up someone's breakfast." Wulf was shaking so hard he nearly fell off his skates. "Scrambled—eggs—bacon—breakfast. Get it?"

"I'm serious, Wulf," said Val. "I think Jinx's wheel bearings are overheating. I should fly over and stop her."

Wulf quieted down. "C'mon, Val," he said. "Bearings don't just overheat by themselves. You've got to be going *way* fast to flame the wheels!"

Val shrugged. "I know it doesn't make sense. All I'm saying is something sounds funny."

"Dude, what do you expect? It's a brand new luge. They all sound funny until they're broken in. Besides, Jinx is no beginner. You know how she hates it when we try to tell her what to do. She's a witch. She can take care of herself."

Wulf had a point. Jinx would never forgive him if he interrupted her first test-drive just because of a suspicious noise. He was also right about another thing: Jinx was a serious athlete. When she wasn't attending spell-casting school or hanging out in Val's garage with her Extreme Monster teammates, she liked nothing better than to go hurtling down a steep hill on a luge. Although she was only twelve, she already enjoyed a growing reputation in California as a skilled luge pilot. She could handle almost any racing challenge thrown at her. Val decided it was probably best to let her find and fix her own bugs.

On this spectacular mid-October morning, Val and Wulf had met Jinx at the track to watch her test-drive her new luge on the sports park's toughest downhill course. Jinx's pet, Bela, was there to cheer on his mistress. Bela was a bat and the Extreme Monsters' unofficial mascot. But unlike the other daring teammates, Bela was timid and nervous. Witnessing Jinx whip around curves at 50 miles per hour often caused him to faint. At the present moment, he was hanging upside down from the guardrail with his wings wrapped tightly over his eyes.

Suddenly, Val was aware that the strange noise had ceased. He stared through his binoculars again. Jinx was ready to roll. She was sitting very still on her luge. Her legs were extended and her feet pointing downhill. Sunlight glinted off the hard plastic visor of her crash helmet. Seconds passed. Jinx leaned forward slowly and placed her palms on the pavement. Then, in a burst of activity, she began pulling herself forward with all her might. The luge squealed, leaped out of the paddle zone, and sped downhill.

"Awesome!" cried Wulf. "She's off to a perfect start."

"I'm not so sure," Val noted worriedly. As soon as Jinx had pushed off, the mystery sputtering noise returned—only this time it was louder.

Val tracked Jinx as she whizzed down the slope. She had shifted into a racing posture to lower her wind resistance. She was now lying flat on her back with her arms at her sides. Her helmeted head rested in a protective cone at the luge's rear. Jinx was gaining speed at a terrific rate. She looked like a blurry silver bullet.

Then it happened.

As Jinx entered the first curve, her luge

began to wobble. The rear end shook, then swung wide. Jinx went skidding across the track, nearly slamming into the barrier. She managed to steer her way back to the inside track. But her luge was fishtailing down the straightaway.

Val flung his Strong-Sites to the ground. "C'mon, Wulf!" he shouted. " Jinx's wheels are seizing up! We've got to reach her before the luge flips."

The hairs on the back of Wulf's neck stiffened. With a low growl, he hopped atop the guardrail in his skates. He clenched his fists in readiness. "She's going to spew a wheel! What's the plan, man?"

Val rose off the ground. "I'll fly over to the luge and grab it from behind," he shouted. "Skate down the track. When Jinx's sled passes by, speed up and grab it from the front. That way, if her wheels go, we can keep her from wiping out. Got it?"

"You bet," Wulf replied.

"W-what about me?" piped up a small, scared voice from under the guardrail.

"Hang in there, Bela. We've got it covered," said Wulf.

By the time the nervous bat had mustered the courage to peek out from under the rail, the two extreme athletes were gone.

Val was streaking through air. His aim was to catch Jinx at the second turn. This nasty hairpin curve marked the approach to Cliffhanger Hill—the steepest slope in the sports park. Val reached the spot as Jinx took the corner. He could see she was trying desperately to slow down. Jinx was sitting up on her board to increase her wind resistance, and leaning into the curve while she braked hard with her heels. But the luge was bouncing so violently that she was finding it impossible to dig into the road. Just then, the luge rocked, went up on two wheels, and nearly tipped over.

Val no longer needed superpowers to figure out what was going on. As Jinx exited the hairpin turn and headed toward Cliffhanger Hill, he saw ribbons of gray smoke trailing from her wheels. He'd been right after all! Something had been sizzling. Jinx's wheels were melting down, and it wouldn't be long before they failed entirely.

Val swooped down and hovered next to Jinx's luge like a jet-fighter escort. Jinx spotted him and gave a wave. Val couldn't tell if she was scared because her face was hidden behind the visor. Pointing toward the underside of the luge, he shouted above the roar, "Your wheels are burning!"

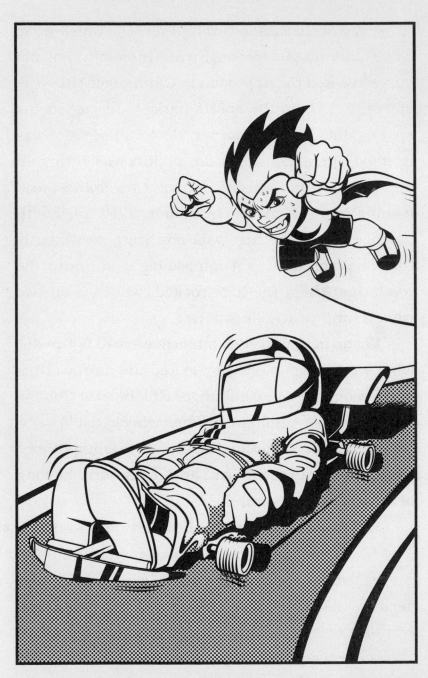

Jinx yelled back through her mask. "Val, my wheels are flaming!"

"I'm going to help you stop!" Val shouted.

"I can't hear you!" she yelled back.

"I said I'm going to help you stop!" Val was screaming at the top of his lungs.

"No use," he sighed. "I'll just have to take it from here."

The luge rocketed down Cliffhanger Hill. Dead ahead, Val sighted Wulf. He was skating down the straightaway, hoping to match Jinx's breakneck pace as she whizzed by. Val flew in closer to the luge and grabbed the end near Jinx's head.

The luge swerved sharply.

"Hey, what are you doing?" Jinx yelled. "Let go of my sled! I'm bringing her in." She raised an arm and tried to push Val away. But Val held on tightly. He began reducing his air speed.

The luge was closing fast on Wulf. He was now only about ten yards ahead, sprinting his heart out.

Jinx lifted her head. She was startled to see the werewolf in the middle of the track. "Wulf—get out of the way!" she screamed. But the skater didn't alter his course.

"Get ready, Wulf!" shouted Val.

As the luge overtook the werewolf, Wulf poured on the speed and edged out in front.

"Now!" cried Val.

Wulf knelt down and gripped the luge near Jinx's feet while Val hit his brakes in mid-air. Bit by bit, the luge began to slow down. It shuddered and shimmied for another 100 yards, and finally came to a halt near the finish line.

Jinx was up off her luge in a flash. She ripped off her helmet and came storming towards Val. Her red eyes were blazing. "What was that all about, you Transylvanian turkey? I ought to turn you into an insect—or a flowerpot. There was no need to play Mr. Hero. I had everything under control."

"Oh, yeah?" said Val. "Then what do you call this?" He picked up her luge and turned it over. Three of its four urethane wheels were melted, the metal trucks twisted all out of shape. He blew on the fourth and it fell off. "If Wulf and I hadn't been holding you up," Val said, "you would have beefed for sure."

Jinx gently nudged another wheel. It dropped off and wobbled away. Her jaw dropped. "I—I didn't notice," she stammered. "I thought—I mean...I'm sorry, Val."

"Forget it," said Val. "It was a close call. But if I were you, I'd get my money back from the place I bought the sled from."

"I hate to tell you this, guys," interrupted Wulf, "but I don't think the luge was the problem."

Val and Jinx turned towards the werewolf in astonishment. Wulf was holding one of the fallen wheels in his hand. He was sniffing it carefully.

"What are you talking about?" asked Jinx.

"This wheel has a strange odor—and I'm not talking about burnt plastic."

"What's it smell like?" Jinx said.

"S-L-I-M-E," spelled out Wulf.

"Slime!" cried Val and Jinx, in mutual horror.

"Exactly," said Wulf. "And you know what that really spells."

"Sabotage," replied Val darkly.

PUZZLE 1

Directions:

Solve the crossword puzzle, then follow the directions below
to discover the first number of your secret code.

ACROSS
1. Type of creature Val is
6. What Wulf smelled in Jinx's wheels
7. This sled-on-wheels is also known as a street _____ .

DOWN
1. Val and his friends live in Monsterey _____.
2. Val's team is known as the Extreme _____.
3. Wulf rides around on in-line _____.
4. She is a witch who likes extreme sports.
5. The fearful bat mascot of the team

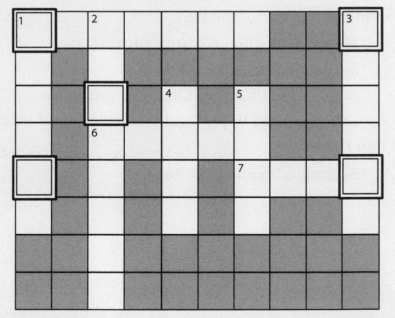

After you've solved the crossword, write the six letters in the boxed
squares down on a piece of paper. When unscrambled, the letters
form a word for a number between one and ten.

Write that number in the CODE KEY on page 91.

18

CHAPTER TWO

Doc Drops a Bombshell

The day after Jinx's meltdown, Val called an emergency meeting of the Extreme Monsters for noon in his garage. Jinx and Bela lived next door, and Wulf's house was just down the block. Steiner and Mumford, the two newest members of the team, lived farther away, in a neighborhood on the other side of Monsterey Valley. They rolled in at around 11:00, Steiner on his BMX bike and Mumford on his skateboard, bearing special treats for everyone. They brought donuts for Jinx, Wulf, and themselves, freeze-dried mosquitoes for Bela, and a six-pack of sparkling beet juice for Val. Coming from a long line of health-conscious, people-friendly vampires, Val was a strict vegetarian. All he drank was beet juice.

****

At 12:00 on the dot, a 30-foot-long vehicle painted with the words

EXTREME MONSTERS
LABORATORY UTILITY VEHICLE

rumbled to a halt in Val's driveway. The L.U.V had an accordion pleat in the middle for making sharp turns. Poking through the roof were wires and hooks, spidery antennas, and several small satellite dishes. In the rear hung metal racks for carrying bikes and other sports equipment.

"Doc's here!" cried Val, lifting the garage door.

A tall, skinny, gray-haired man with big ears and a banana-sized moustache stood in the driveway. Strapped on his back was a knapsack full of high-tech gear. Doc, the Monsters' coach, was an all-round technical wizard. He strode into the garage and asked solemnly, "Where's the patient?"

"Over there," said Jinx, pointing to the damaged luge on Val's workbench.

Doc began his examination. He put on a pair of thick, wire-rimmed eyeglasses. The wire frames went over his ears and around the back of his head, where they merged with a short, spiral electrical cord. Doc reached back and plugged the end of the cord into an outlet in his knapsack. His lenses blinked on. They gave off a powerful, green, laser-like light.

"Mr. Doc? What are those?" a muffled voice asked shyly. The question came from Mumford. He was the youngest member of the Extreme Monsters and their main speed-climber.

Val glanced at Mumford with surprise. He hadn't heard the little guy speak in all day. Mumford was something of a puzzle. When he'd first joined the team, he was covered from head to toe with bandages. Months had passed, but the bandages never came off. Nobody on the team had any idea what Mumford actually looked like.

Everyone figured that Mumford was a mummy because of the bandages and the weird Egyptian markings on his outfits. But he claimed to be only nine years old—which didn't make much sense if he was a mummy.

Val and Jinx were worried about him. Mumford was constantly getting injured and needing even more bandages! They suggested that he might want to consider taking up a safer sport. But Mumford wouldn't change. It was obvious that his dream was to become an Extreme Monster. Val and Jinx were his role models.

Though they worried about him, Val and Jinx also saw great potential in Mumford. They believed that with training and time, he could become an extraordinary member of the team. But they promised each other they'd help Mumford improve his climbing so that he wouldn't get hurt so much.

"This is my Electro-Optical Atomic De-Obfuscator, son," replied Doc to Mumford's question, as he studied the wheel bearings. "It will tell me, lickety-split, if Jinx's luge was sabotaged."

Doc unplugged his E.O.A.D.O. glasses and set them down on the bench. "Well, there's no doubt about it," he said. "Jinx's bearings were sabotaged. They were coated with a thin film of motion-activated thermal slime. The moment she moved her luge, the slime began to sizzle—like bacon in a pan. The faster her luge went, the hotter the slime got. The urethane wheels and the bearings melted."

"Figures," said Val, plunking himself down in his favorite chair, next to his trophies. "There's only one person I know who uses slime as a weapon of mess destruction—Damon Christopher."

The mention of that name sent a shudder through the group. Damon Christopher was the president of Pendant Enterprises, a billion-dollar company that manufactured extreme sports gear. He was also the owner and manager of Team Pendant. Team Pendant was a highly successful sports club, the top team on the gravity circuit in which the Extreme Monsters competed.

Although Team Pendant had an incredible won-lost record and a lineup of League superstars, the Extreme Monsters had become convinced that many of Pendant's greatest victories had been achieved through cheating. The problem, as the Extreme Monsters saw it, was the team's owner. Damon Christopher had a reputation as one of the wealthiest, greediest, meanest, and slimiest operators around. His goal was to make Pendant the top name in extreme sports, and he was not going to let anyone—or anything—stand in his way. Not rules and regulations. Not standards of fair play. Not public opinion. And certainly not his sworn enemies, the Extreme Monsters.

Christopher and the Extreme Monsters had a history of unpleasant run-ins. He had held a grudge against Val and his teammates since they had beaten Team Pendant in the Big Sur Extreme Nationals, televised on the Satellite Extreme Sports Channel. Damon Christopher had foolishly bragged to the press beforehand that Pendant sports gear would make his athletes unbeatable. Team Pendant's stunning upset at the hands of the Extreme Monsters left him fuming. His anger worsened after he became the butt of a few jokes on the late-night television comedy circuit.

During the annual Extreme Dream-Team Olympics, Val and Wulf had exposed some of the Christopher gang's dirty tricks. Team Pendant was kicked out of the contest. In interviews with reporters afterward, Damon maintained that he and his team were innocent of any wrongdoing. His athletes had been "framed," he said, by jealous opponents. He didn't name names, but made it clear that he felt the Extreme Monsters were to blame.

The greatest blow to Damon's ego came a year later when Doc, who'd been employed as Pendant's chief scientist and genius-in-residence, had defected to the Extreme Monsters, taking Steiner with him. Steiner had been Team Pendant's bicycle motocross ace and its fastest-rising star until, with the help of Val and the Extreme Monsters, he was able to escape Christopher's clutches. When it became clear that Steiner was an orphan without a home, Doc took him in.

With the additions of Doc as coach and the fearless Steiner on BMX, the Extreme Monsters suddenly emerged, in the eyes of many sports fans, as a world-class team. The bitterly resentful Damon Christopher could neither forget nor forgive this loss.

"There's one thing I don't get, Doc," Wulf said abruptly. "How was Damon able to slime Jinx's luge in the first place? It was brand new."

Doc turned to Jinx. "Where'd you buy it?"

"Online at x-quipment.com."

"There's your answer, Wulf," replied Doc. "Damon Christopher secretly bought the company a month ago. He must have found out that Jinx was a customer. When she ordered her new luge, he just had one of his stooges dip its wheels in thermal slime before they shipped it out."

Jinx looked puzzled. "But why?"

Doc's expression grew grave. He glanced around the garage. "I think the answer's obvious, my friends. Damon is getting desperate. The popularity of Team Pendant has dipped. Pendant's

sales are dropping, too. You have showed him up enough times, and he needs a victory badly—a big victory. Ring any bells?"

"Duh!" exclaimed Jinx, slapping her forehead.

"What was I thinking? Damon wants to weaken us for the Howl-O-Ween Games. It's the biggest event of the year around here."

"Exactly," said Doc. "He's tried cheating and cutting corners *during* competitions—and failed miserably. Now he's trying to cheat *before* a major competition, when the judge isn't looking. He wants revenge, and he'll stop at nothing to destroy us as a team. We need to be extra careful from here on in. Your safety is paramount."

Doc paused and took a deep breath. "This, unfortunately, brings me around to the second—and least happy—reason I stopped by today."

"What's the problem, Doc?" Val asked, rising from his chair.

"You're not going to like this."

"Try us, we're tough," replied Wulf, flexing both arms.

"It concerns the Howl-O-Ween Games."

"What about them?" Jinx asked.

Doc sighed. "For the safety of the team, I'm suggesting we pull out of the event. In fact, tomorrow I'm going to ask the League to cancel the games."

"W-H-A-A-A-T!!!" moaned the Extreme Monsters together.

"No way!" cried Wulf. He stamped his in-lines defiantly. The force of his powerful legs caused the whole garage to shake.

PUZZLE 2

Directions:

Check off whether the following statements are true (T) or false (F), then follow the directions below to discover the next four letters of your secret code.

	T	F
A. Doc once worked for Damon Christopher.		
B. Jinx bought her new street luge in a department store.		
C. Mumford has an annoying habit of talking too much.		
D. Steiner was the Extreme Monsters' in-line skating ace.		

Place whatever T's or F's you have checked off in the secret code boxes provided on page 91.

CHAPTER THREE

Once in a Blue Moon

The Extreme Monsters were in an uproar. The Howl-O-Ween Games were the sports event of the year in Monsterey Valley. A five-hour festival of X contests and entertainment, the celebration combined Halloween glamour and glitz with extreme thrills and chills. No fan was admitted without a Halloween costume. Competitions always paused at midnight for a costume parade and rock concert. This year the featured act was The Numb Skulls, the hottest zombie-metal band in the world.

The Extreme Monsters were looking forward to the games for weeks. It was unthinkable that they would have to withdraw from the competition. The monsters all shouted their protests at once—except Val. No one was willing to let anyone else speak.

Val saw that Doc was losing his patience. Minutes passed, but the hubbub showed no sign of ending. Doc wheeled around abruptly and strode toward his L.U.V.

"Wait, Doc—don't leave!" cried Val.

"Who said anything about leaving?" Doc called back. "I'm going to print something out from my computer. It's the only way I can persuade you kids of the seriousness of my request." He disappeared into the vehicle.

Val knew he had only a few minutes to get his friends back into line. He raised two fingers to his lips and blew hard.

Phweeeeeeeeeeeeeet!!

The Extreme Monsters fell silent. Val quickly gathered everyone round. This time the discussion of a pullout went smoothly. All of the monsters—except Bela—strongly opposed skipping the games.

"We can't pull out," declared Wulf. "It's against the Monster Code of Honor."

Jinx looked at Wulf and rolled her eyes.

"There's no such thing as the Monster Code of Honor," she said.

"Well, there should be," shrugged Wulf.

"Halloween is the one day of the year when everyone can find out how much fun it is to be a monster," added Steiner, his voice choking with emotion. "How would it look if the Extreme Monsters didn't show?"

"I'll bet it's Damon Christopher and his Pendant goons! Someone ought to put a stop to that menace," Wulf muttered.

"And I know who's just the witch to do it," said Jinx. With that, she snapped her fingers. A magic wand appeared out of thin air. Before anyone could stop her, she'd grabbed it and begun chanting:

Smelly hemlock,

Lawn unmowed.

Lizard's lost sock,

Mucky road.

Make Damon Christopher

A creeping t—

"Stop, Jinx!—Don't finish that spell!" Val cried out. He reached over and yanked the wand from her hand. "You know the rules! No black magic—ever!"

Jinx folded her arms across her chest. "Party pooper!" she grumped. "Nobody stopped Damon from ruining my luge. He deserves to be turned into a toad."

"Toad's too good for him, Jinx," quipped Wulf. "Make him a dust bunny." He grinned as he skated lazy figure eights in front of Val's workbench.

Val rolled his eyes. "No toads! No dust bunnies! No nothing! We don't turn people into creatures or...or...*things*—not even the bad guys."

"Ahem!" Doc cleared his throat loudly. "Are you all quite finished?" He was standing in the middle of the garage, clutching what looked like a rolled-up poster.

Val stepped forward nervously. "We've been talking, Doc," he said, "and we just can't agree with you. We've decided it would be wrong to withdraw from the games just because of Damon."

Doc raised his eyebrows. "Who said anything about Damon Christopher?" he said. "I would never ask you to pull out just because of *his* shenanigans."

"But you said—"

"I got to say precious little, if you remember," Doc remarked tartly. "You kids were doing all the talking—and jumping to extremely wild conclusions, I might add."

Jinx spoke up. "But if Damon isn't the problem, Doc, then who is?"

"Not *who*, Jinx—*what*."

The Extreme Monsters glanced back and forth at each other in puzzlement.

"Look, it's easier for me to show you than to explain," Doc said. He unrolled the poster on Val's workbench.

"I don't get it," blurted out Steiner. "It's a picture of the earth surrounded by a swarm of blue moons."

"Right you are, my boy!" Doc said. "What you see here are all the known occurrences of a blue moon over the last three centuries."

"C'mon, Doc," Val said, "There's no such thing as a blue moon. It's just an expression. It means something rare."

"Right," noted Jinx, "as in, 'once in a blue moon'.

"Oh yes, there is such a thing," Doc replied. "It's a very real, though rare, event. Whenever two full moons appear in a single month, the second is called a "blue moon." Doc traced a finger across the diagram in a big arc. "As you can see from the chart, a blue moon occurs about once every three years. But this Halloween"—his finger halted on the darkest blue circle—"the planets and stars are going to line up in a freakish way to produce the rarest and most dangerous kind of blue moon."

"Which is?" asked Steiner.

"The Devil's Blue Moon."

Bela gulped so hard it sounded as if he'd swallowed his feet.

"Okay, let's suppose this...this Devil's Blue Moon is real," said Wulf. "I still don't see what it has to do with us or the Howl-O-Ween Games."

"You're just the right guy to ask that question, Wulf," replied Doc.

"*Me?* Gee, thanks, Doc," said Wulf, extremely pleased with himself. Then his expression changed. "Hey, wait a minute. Why me?"

Doc ran his eyes around the group. "You know how all of you, as monsters, are affected by the phases of the moon."

The six Extreme Monsters nodded. "Wulf here, for example, goes...well...a little loony during a full moon."

"Do not!" Wulf objected.

"Do, too!" said Jinx.

"You're not immune either, Jinx," Doc scolded. "Full moons always crank your spells up to extra-strength." Doc paused. "I could go on about Val's lunar headaches and Steiner's muscle cramps. You all get the point, though. A full moon is nothing but trouble for monsters."

"Am I missing something, Doc?" Val asked, scratching his head. "All monsters I know use the moonscreen you invented. Just a dab on the skin and the full moon's no problem."

"This time it will be," Doc said. He directed everyone's attention to the diagram. "Neither a full moon nor a blue moon has any effect on humans," he explained. "But it's a different story for a monster."

Doc took a pen and circled some figures at the bottom. "Consider these facts," he said. "The rays of a full or blue moon boost the typical monster's powers five times. But a blue moon on Halloween is two times stronger than that...and a Devil's Blue Moon is fifty times stronger than that...and a Devil's Blue Moon on Halloween is two times stronger than that. By my calculations, the powers of all unprotected monsters at the Howl-O-Ween Games—"

"— could increase 1,000 times!" blurted Val, staggering backwards.

"Could that really happen?" asked Steiner.

"I'm afraid so," Doc said. "On Halloween, the moon will rise full and gradually turn blue. It will stay blue for precisely thirteen minutes and thirteen seconds. Then it will fade back to white. What will happen during that time is anyone's guess. But I don't want any of you to be caught outdoors when it occurs."

"Won't the League's Neutralizer Wristbands protect us?" Jinx asked.

Neutralizer Wristbands were special devices all monsters wore during extreme sports events. The wristbands absorbed and temporarily neutralized any magic powers a monster might have. It was the only way monsters and humans, who'd been living and working together side by side for generations, could compete together fairly in the same events.

Doc gazed at Jinx and shook his head. "The Neutralizers can only handle energy fields up to ten times normal—not 1,000. The sheer power of a blue moon will cause their chips to blow like overloaded electrical circuits."

"You mean sparks?" Mumford asked quietly.

"I mean huge ones, son," said Doc. "They'd make a lightning storm look tame."

"What about your moonscreen?" asked Val.

"My present formula doesn't work against blue-moon rays," Doc replied. "I've been working on a new formula, but I haven't had any luck so far. And time is running out."

"What about the League? Does it know anything about this?" asked Wulf.

"I'm meeting with the League president tomorrow," Doc said. "I'm going to present my findings and request a delay." He scanned the faces of the Extreme Monsters. "I'd like to take a few of you along with me. Your opinions carry a lot of weight in the League. Maybe together we can persuade them to avert a disaster."

Val pursed his lips. He turned toward his teammates and said, "This emergency goes way beyond our personal feelings. Every monster at the games could be in danger. I move we change our votes and support Doc's request for a delay."

"Agreed!" shouted the monsters in unison.

"Then it's settled, Doc," said Val. "We're behind you 100 percent. How about if Jinx and Wulf and I go down with you to League headquarters?"

"Perfect," said Doc. He smiled for the first time since he'd arrived. "Our meeting starts at 11:00 a.m. I'll pick you up at 10:00."

Just then there was a sound of large wings beating the air. Two long, black feathers spiraled gently down toward the driveway.

The Extreme Monsters ran outside and gazed toward the roof of the garage. A black bird had taken off and was flying away at great speed over the neighboring housetops.

"Anybody see what kind of bird it was?" asked Wulf.

"A raven," came a muffled voice from above.

Val looked up. Mumford was sitting on top of his oak tree. Somehow the little guy had managed to untie a line of his bandages. He'd tossed one end over the highest limb and climbed up the makeshift rope in matter of seconds.

"I'll bet it was Damon's raven, Vincent," said Steiner. "He was probably spying on us right from the beginning."

Val gave a weary sigh. At that moment, he couldn't tell which emotion he felt more strongly—sadness at having to give up the Howl-O-Ween Games, anger at Vincent's spying, or wonder at the secret talents of the young Mumford.

PUZZLE 3

Directions:

In this chapter Doc tells the Extreme Monsters that the moon is going to create a big problem for monsters at the upcoming Howl-O-Ween Games. Below you'll find descriptions of different types of moons. Pick the one that Doc says is most dangerous for monsters

A.   Full moon

B.   Half-moon on Halloween

C.   Blue moon

D.   Crescent moon

E.   Man-in-the-moon blue moon

F.   Halloween crescent moon

G.   Harvest moon on Halloween

H.   New Moon on New Year's Day

I.   Horned moon

J.   Devil's blue moon on Halloween

K.   Ring-around-the-moon

Write the letter for the correct answer in the secret code box provided on page 91.

CHAPTER FOUR

"T. Rex," for Short

The words painted on the door in big, gold-leaf letters read:

CENTRAL HEADQUARTERS
EXTREME TEAM SPORTS LEAGUE (ETSL)
T. REXFORD SNATTLY,
PRESIDENT & CHIEF EXTREME OFFICER

Doc walked inside with Val, Jinx, and Wulf close behind. Under his arm he carried a laptop computer that held a slide show featuring blue moon diagrams and calculations. A chestnut-haired woman was sitting behind the reception desk doing a crossword puzzle. She was dressed in a stylish skating outfit that included Day-Glo elbow and knee pads and a jazzy, matching crash helmet.

"Good morning, Daisy," said Doc. "That's got to be your nicest outfit yet."

"Hi, Doc. Thanks!" replied Daisy, flashing him

a friendly smile. "You have an appointment with Mr. Snattly."

"Yes, and I've brought the Extreme Monsters. It's their first time here."

"You brought the Extreme Monsters?" squealed the receptionist happily. "Mr. Snattly didn't say anything about *that.*" She craned her neck to get a glimpse of the super-athletes bunched up behind Doc.

"Well, I brought three of them," said the scientist.

Daisy dropped her puzzle and pencil and grabbed a marking pen. "Now don't any of you move!" she said. She rolled her chair back and rose to her feet with a loud clatter. Val noticed she was wearing skates. "I'm a huge, huge fan," she said, rolling around to the front of the desk. "I saw you at the Global Games. You came from behind. You guys were awesome!" She tilted her head toward the trio, handed Val the pen, and said, "Could you sign my crash helmet?"

"Er...sure," said Val, taking the marker.

After the three monsters had finished signing Daisy's helmet, Val looked again and noticed that the helmet had also been signed by Chip Brentwood and Scott Squire, two of the human stars of Team Pendant. The young receptionist straightened up, beaming. "Follow me," she said. "Mr. Snattly is expecting you."

Daisy escorted the four visitors down a long corridor. Pausing at the corner office, she poked her head inside.

"It's Doc, Mr. Snattly, and"—she smiled happily—"three Extreme Monsters."

"Excellent. Have them come in, Daisy," called a gravelly voice from within. "We're all waiting for them."

"*We?*" Doc whispered to Val. "I wonder who *we* is? It was supposed to be *him* and *us.*"

When the Extreme Monsters entered the League president's spacious office, they got a nasty surprise.

"It's *him!*" hissed Jinx into Val's ear.

Damon Christopher was standing beside President Snattly's desk. He was sporting a black suit, a maroon silk tie, and fancy shoes. He wore a grin so wide and fake it looked like it had been pasted onto his face.

Damon was holding a laser pointer aimed at a nearby screen, on which a large chart was displayed. At the back of the room, operating the computer and projector that beamed the image on the screen, were the billionaire's two henchmen—Cletus and Clem Sline. Val also noticed that Chip and Scott were seated at the back of the room lookng bored. Scott nodded to Val, who nodded back.

Cletus and Clem were two brothers with talents for extreme sports and extreme mischief. Damon had discovered them surfing on jet boards in a polluted swamp. He'd signed them on the spot to race for Team Pendant. Tall, green, and warty, the geeky pair were monsters endowed with great strength. They also had a unique, creepy ability to make their bodies ooze and spray different kinds of slime. Everyone knew them by their nickname—the Slime Brothers.

Val figured out in a split second that they were the source of the thermal slime that had ruined Jinx's luge. Jinx made a sudden move as if to snap her fingers and fetch her wand.

"Don't even think about it!" Val muttered under his breath. Jinx gave Val a dark look, but heeded his warning.

A short man shaped like a teakettle with two spouts for arms waddled toward them with a big smile.

"Doc," the man said, "how nice to see you again." He took Doc's hand and pumped it hard. Then he turned toward the Extreme Monsters and stretched out his arms. "Guys, guys, guys—what can I say? I've heard so much about you, but I don't believe we've ever met. T. Rexford Snattly. You can call me T. Rex, for short."

"Funny, you don't look like a T. Rex," snorted Wulf. "Get it?—T. Rex—tall dinosaur—*short guy?*"

Val gave his clueless buddy a sharp poke in the ribs. "Don't mind Wulf," he said, turning beet-juice red. "He means well, but he says things without thinking. We're all very pleased to meet you."

T. Rex laughed heartily. "No offense taken. I am short." He slapped Wulf on the back. "I like a werewolf with a sense of humor." He waddled back toward his desk and motioned for his four visitors to join him. "I want you to meet my other guests." Doc and the Monsters had little choice but to follow.

T. Rex stood smiling between Damon Christopher and the Extreme Monsters. He seemed unaware of how intensely bitter their rivalry had become. "You know Damon Christopher, I'm sure," he said. "These are his associates, Clem and Cletus Slime—er—Sline."

The Extreme Monsters nodded politely. Damon nodded back. No one offered to shake hands. After an awkward silence, T. Rex invited Doc and the Monsters to take seats in a semicircle in front of the projector screen. Damon and the brothers remained standing.

"I understand you're here to discuss the Howl-O-Ween Games?" T. Rex said to Doc.

"Yes, I—"

"The games are going to be incredible this year—our best ever!"

"That's exactly what I wanted to—"

"Damon here has been handling all the business and technical details," T. Rex breezed on. "Doing a super job. He's arranged to have the games televised on the Satellite Extreme Sports Channel. We're talking global feed here. That means mega exposure for our League."

"But T. Rex, that's just what we need to discuss," Doc managed to slip in.

"Of course we do," said T. Rex. "Hold that thought,

though. I want you hear what Damon has planned. You're going to love it. Tell them, Damon."

Doc slumped back in his chair and sighed quietly.

Damon Christopher gave a toss of his heavily gelled hair. Then he turned on his artificially sweetened smile. "It's just like T. Rex says," he began. "We're talking mega-mega TV coverage. That's 10 satellite feeds, 40 countries, 200 million viewers—monsters and humans alike. We're booking top-of-the-line superstars for the midnight gig. Tom and Paris and Jennifer and Jason are coming. Angelina, Brad, and Jessica are leaning. And Justin, Ashlee, and Britney are solid maybes."

"Fabulous, Damon," remarked the president.

"You can say that again, T. Rex," said Damon, with a sly wink at the Monsters. "An opportunity like this doesn't come along often—maybe once in a *blue moon.*"

At the mention of these words, Val nearly fell off his seat. He glanced at Doc and his teammates. They'd all been taken by surprise. There was no way Damon could have let that slip by accident. Damon's spy, Vincent, must have told him something about Doc's discovery. But how much did Damon know?

Val decided it was time to find out. "What's in this for you, Mr. Christopher?" he blurted out.

Damon looked hurt by the question. "For me?" he said. "Almost nothing. I'll be happy just knowing that the League is finally getting the exposure it deserves."

"*Really!*" said Val, with an edge to his voice. "I read in *Xtreme Sports News* that your company is supplying all the satellite dishes and refreshments. I also heard that only one company—yours—is allowed to sell sports gear at the games."

Damon smiled. "And why not? My products are the best."

"I also heard that Pendant is going to be the only television advertiser."

"What's your point?" Damon snapped, suddenly annoyed.

"I'm not sure what you're saying, either," observed T. Rex. "I agreed to let Pendant do everything. Damon has assured me it would make things go smoother."

Val turned toward the League president. "My point is simple, sir," he said. "Mr. Christopher stands to make a lot of money if the games succeed and lose a lot if they're postponed."

"Postponed?" T. Rex said, with a nervous laugh. "No way! The weather forecast is perfect for Halloween."

"But the moon forecast isn't!" Doc broke in. He flipped opened his briefcase and slapped a printout of the slide show on the desk.

"What are these?" asked T. Rex.

"Our big, blue headache," said Doc.

For the next hour, Doc patiently went over his findings with the League president. During that time,

Damon didn't say a thing, a fact that Val found both strange and suspicious. When Doc finally finished his presentation, T. Rex Snattly's eyes could hardly focus. He had the look of a drowning man hoping someone would throw him a lifeline. He turned to Damon and moaned, "What do you make of this?"

Damon straightened his tie. He threw back his shoulders. Then he flicked on his pointer and his oily smile. "Last chart, boys!" he said. The Slime twins clicked through Damon's slides until a chart labeled THE MYTH OF THE DEVIL'S BLUE MOON appeared.

The Extreme Monsters gasped.

"A little bird told me about Doc's crazy theory," Damon began, smirking. "We know about full moons and blue moons and their effect on monsters. But this crackpot theory about a Devil's Blue Moon is totally unbelievable. I understand Doc's worries, I truly do, but I would have thought that, as a man of science, he would not have been duped by this...old wives' tale. I think when I'm finished, you'll see that Doc is...more than a little confused, shall we say."

"Liar!" shouted Wulf.

"Quiet!" ordered Snattly. "I'm in charge here. Continue, Damon."

With words T. Rex found instantly reassuring, Damon attacked Doc's points one by one. There was no such thing as a blue moon, he said. Had anyone ever seen a news report about a blue moon? No. Was any scientist other than Doc jumping up and down about it? No. Was the Internet buzzing with blue-moon talk? No. If the Howl-O-Ween Games were postponed for such an insane reason, he said, the ETSL would be the laughingstock of the sports world.

When Damon concluded, T. Rex jumped up and hugged him. "Thank you, Damon, for setting things straight. The games will go on," he said. "I won't delay them one second for such loony nonsense."

The Extreme Monsters were numb. Even Doc seemed stunned. Damon had outsmarted them. Val could see that he was filled with joy at his victory. On his face was a sly, mocking grin.

PUZZLE 4

Directions:

Look at the drawings below. Only one could possibly be of the receptionist, Daisy, at the Extreme Team Sports League headquarters. Use what you know from reading this chapter to pick the right drawing.

A.

B.

C.

D.

E.

***Then write your answer in the secret code box
provided on page 91.***

CHAPTER FIVE

Mist Opportunity

"Don't look now, but we're being followed," Val informed Steiner and Mumford calmly.

"Uh-oh, that means trouble!" muttered Steiner.

"No, it doesn't," said Val. "I've been waiting for a chance like this for days."

"Huh?" said Steiner, doing a double take.

Val just smiled at him mysteriously. A clever plan was hatching in his brain on that beautiful, sunny morning.

The Extreme Monsters had just turned onto Main Street. The three teammates were making their way slowly back to Val's place after visiting Doc and Steiner's house on the other side of town. Val was riding his skateboard. Steiner was pedaling his BMX beside him. And Mumford was skitching. He had lashed one of his bandages around Steiner's seat, and was using it as a tow rope to pull himself along on a skateboard.

More than a week had passed since the Extreme Monsters had had their disastrous meeting with T. Rexford Snattly. The Howl-O-Ween Games were now just two days away. All this time Doc had been working frantically on developing a new moonscreen formula—one that he hoped would protect monsters from the harmful effects of blue-moon rays. Earlier this morning he'd called Val excitedly to say that he'd finally made a breakthrough. The first batch of his MPF 1313 (Moon Protection Formula, #1313) was ready! A second batch—large enough to shield 100 more monsters—was in the works.

Doc had asked Val to hurry over and pick up the first samples. With this new, improved formula, he'd said, the Extreme Monsters could participate in the games safely. And if weird things did happen when the moon started turning blue, they would be able to snap into action and rescue moonstruck victims.

Now, as the three friends cruised through town, six shiny tubes—one for each Extreme Monster, including Bela—lay tucked away in Steiner's saddlebags.

"Are you *sure* we're being followed?" Steiner asked.

"Positive," Val replied. "I spotted Clem Sline diving behind a mailbox when we left your house. He's been tailing us on his Whisperboard ever since."

The Whisperboard was a stealth skateboard invented by Doc when he'd worked for Damon. It had a miniature jet-powered engine that enabled it to go as fast as a race car. Because it made no noise, Damon's henchmen used it for spying.

"Where is he now?" Steiner said, twisting around for a look.

"Don't turn your head!" Val ordered. "I don't want Clem to know we're on to him yet." He increased his board's speed and signaled to Steiner to keep pace. "Damon has been spying on us long enough," he continued. "It's time we turned the tables on him."

"What do you mean?" Steiner asked.

"Look," Val explained, "Damon's no dope. He knows Doc isn't some crackpot scientist and that the blue-moon effect is real. But he did everything he could last week to make sure the games went on. Why?"

"It's obvious. You've said it yourself. He's greedy."

Val hopped the curb and rode it for a while, grinding his back axle and sending sparks flying. "So true," he said, jumping back into the street. "But my vampire's instinct tells me it's something bigger. I bet he's got some huge scam planned for the games. Everyone there could be in danger. We've got to find out what he's up to."

"But how?" Steiner asked. "And why is having a goon like Clem on our tail a good thing?"

"Because I'm going to trick him into leading me directly to Damon," Val replied.

"Unh-uh. N-no way!" Steiner exclaimed. "You are not going to try to sneak inside Pendant Enterprises."

"In fact, I am," declared Val.

Steiner became upset. "I can't let you do this. I know what goes on inside those gates. I once rode for Team Pendant, remember? Damon kept me locked up. I'd still be there if you guys hadn't won my contract. I won't let that happen to you."

"Don't worry," said Val, with a mischievous

smile. "I've got a few monster-tricks up my sleeve. With a little luck, Damon will never know I'm spying on him."

"With a little luck?" cried Steiner, swerving to avoid a jaywalker. "Are you crazy? You can't do this alone. I'm going with you."

"Me, too," mumbled Mumford .

"Sorry, guys," Val said. "This job has to be solo. Besides, I'm counting on both of you to get Doc's tubes safely back to my house. I'm positive that's what Clem is after. We can't let Doc's formula fall into Damon's hands. That's top priority." He looked Steiner straight in the eyes. "Now do you understand why we have to split up?"

"I guess so," said Steiner grudgingly, "but that doesn't mean I have to like it."

Val shifted his position on the board so that he was facing Mumford. "Pass me your knapsack," he said. "I want Clem to think you're handing over the tubes." Mumford obligingly slipped off his pack and gave it to Val, who quickly strapped it on.

As the three Extreme Monsters rode past the main shopping block, Val gazed over at Steiner and said, "Here's the plan. At the next corner, you hang a hard right. Duck into Joe's Garage. I'll turn left and head for the big construction site. Clem will have to make a choice. I'm sure he'll follow me. When he does, you and Mumford head back to my house. Call everybody on your cell and tell them to meet you there—Doc, too. I'll see you in a couple of hours."

"Good luck, Val," Steiner called as the teammates parted in opposite directions.

Val glanced back over his shoulder. It was just as he'd thought. Clem Sline had hung left at the corner and was now in open pursuit. Val veered off the road and started down a shallow ditch toward the construction site. Clem took the detour, too. Val's wheels clattered as he bumped down the rough surface. At the end of the ditch was a long wooden ramp that sloped down into the construction area. Work on the building was still in its early stages. The structure had concrete floors but no walls, and all the steel beams and girders were still exposed, like bones on a skeleton.

As he neared the end of the ramp, Val sped up and hunched down low, stretching out his arms for balance. At the last second he sprang up out of his crouch, performing a perfect Ollie. He snapped down the tail of his board and soared high into the air. Just to show off, Val hit a 360, spinning all the way around before touching down. He landed gracefully on the concrete slab of the first floor.

The Slime Brother was right behind. He grinned a slimy smile at Val. He came shooting down the ramp, his legs bent deeply at the knees. Uncoiling, Clem nailed the aerial, too. As soon as his wheels hit concrete, he kicked his board into hyperdrive. He was closing in fast.

Val noticed a long iron pipe poking down at an angle through a big hole in the floor above. The pipe was about as thick as a goal post—just wide enough to ride. Val put on a tremendous burst of speed and made for it. With his super hearing, Val could hear Clem's rolling not far behind, but he wasn't fazed. Val was really in the zone now. He knew he would soon be quite literally untouchable.

Just before the pipe, Val Ollied onto the railing and rode a 50/50 grind straight up the incline. As he streaked through the opening, he executed a perfect kick flip. The board spun in the air and landed upright on the floor above.

Seconds later, Clem rocketed through the opening himself. He popped a monstrous Ollie and flew up all five steps in one leap. He reached the

top of the stairs hoping to resume the chase, but Val was nowhere to be seen. His skateboard was sitting abandoned by the edge of the hole. Clem searched the entire floor methodically and then the entire construction site, but his quarry had simply...*disappeared.* Clem scratched his head, mystified. He hadn't seen Val fly away or try to steal past him. But he wasn't hiding anywhere in the building, either. Dejected at his failure to intercept the Extreme Monsters' captain, Clem hopped on his whisperboard and headed back to report to Damon.

If Clem had been a brighter or more observant monster, he might have noticed a faint thread of mist clinging to the end of his board as he snaked through the traffic. Unfortunately, Clem was neither bright nor observant. And so, about half an hour later, when Clem and his whisperboard passed through the heavily guarded gates of Pendant Enterprises, so did the almost-invisible wisp of mist.

Val was in!

Damon Christopher was standing in front of a projector screen again, laser pointer in hand. This time he was making a presentation to his henchmen and the members of Team Pendant. The site was Pendant Enterprises' "war room," a secure, windowless communications center in the heart of the sub-sub-basement of the Pendant Towers Building.

"Listen up," Damon was saying. "I have fabulous news. In just two days we are going to win the Howl-O-Ween Games. Not just one event—all of them! Even better, in just two days the Extreme Monsters will cease to be a threat to us. On Halloween we will gain the power to make Team Pendant the greatest sports team in the history of the world."

As Damon's audience stood up and cheered, shivers went up and down Val's misty spine.

"Now here's how we're going to pull it off," said Damon. He flashed his pointer on a chart. "We'll have ten satellite dishes arranged in a circle around the Extreme Sports Park. Two will send live video of the games to the world. But secretly, the rest will be capturing precious blue-moon rays." He paused. "Do you have any idea what this means?"

The members of his audience looked blank.

"Anyone? No one? Okay. Well, the answer's simple. A monster exposed to blue-moon rays instantly becomes a super-monster—stronger, faster, more magical. But, best of all, a Neutralizer Wristband can't cancel that advantage. So a team with a secret supply of blue energy can cheat and cheat and cheat and nobody will be the wiser. Isn't that fantastic?" He grinned wickedly.

"You bet!" screamed the Slime Brothers.

Damon grinned again. "Doc and I are the only people who really understand the significance of blue-moon rays. And last week I knocked Doc and the Extreme Monsters out of the picture. You know what that means?"

Again, blank stares.

"No one can stop us!"

His audience applauded strongly.

"On Halloween," Damon continued, "I intend to download enough blue energy to last our team a century. And once I do, Team Pendant will be unbeatable. Just watch, companies everywhere will be begging each of you to do TV commercials."

At this, Damon's henchmen went wild.

Val had heard enough. He drifted slowly toward the air vent, through a grate, and out a duct into a kinder, saner world.

PUZZLE 5

Directions:

Clem Slime is chasing Val around the construction site. Only one path leads out of the maze. Help Val find the correct escape route.

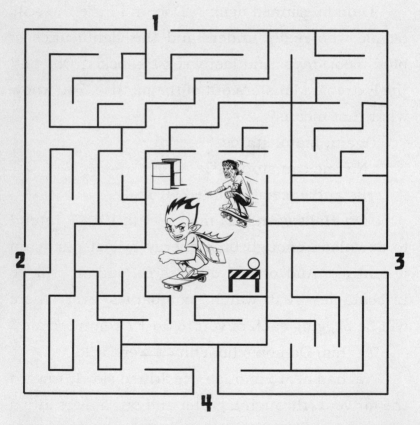

Mark the letter of the correct exit in the secret code box provided on page. 91.

HOWL-O-WEEN GAMES

CHAPTER SIX

Let the Games Begin!

"So that's his game!" Doc exclaimed. "Damon thinks he can store blue-moon energy like electricity in a battery."

It was mid-afternoon, and Doc and the Extreme Monsters had gathered at Val's garage as the team captain had requested. An unsmiling Val had just finished telling the story of what he'd learned inside Damon's war room.

"Is it possible?" asked Jinx. She cracked open a box containing two foam bumpers for her new replacement luge. "Can Damon use satellite dishes to download blue-moon rays?"

"I'm afraid so, Jinx," Doc said. He did some fast arithmetic. "With eight dishes, he could harvest enough blue energy to last his team a century."

"Then I guess we're sunk," said Steiner. "Team Pendant is going to have the best extreme athlete lineup in the world. With super-monsters and human superstars like Brentwood and Squire, they'll be way better than us!" He kicked the pedal of his BMX bike in frustration. "The League might as well crown Damon the King of Extreme."

"I wouldn't go that far," Doc replied. "I think our friend Damon could be in for a few nasty surprises."

"What do you mean?" Val asked.

"I've been doing some research," Doc said. "My calculations show that blue-moon energy is incredibly strange stuff. The harder you try to cram it into a small space, the harder it resists."

"Are you saying it, like, *pushes back?*" said Jinx.

"Exactly. It's very springy."

"Hmm," said Val, thinking out loud. "So if Damon tries to force too much blue energy into his battery..."

"It could literally explode, or simply go *pffffffft!* and melt away like cotton candy in a rainstorm."

"Sheeesh!" exclaimed Wulf.

"But, to be honest with all of you," Doc went

on, "I'm far less concerned about Damon's battery melting down than I am about our biggest blue-moon mystery."

"Which is?" asked Jinx.

"What's going to happen during the games when the Neutralizer Wristbands overload and blow?"

"You still think they'll blow, Doc?" wondered Steiner

"Sky high," said Doc. "There's no doubt about it. The neutralizers weren't made to absorb such a sudden surge in monster powers."

"And when they do?" questioned Val.

"Everyone in the park—humans and monsters alike—will be zapped with weird magical forces."

"Sounds totally wild, dudes," said Wulf.

"Way wild," Doc replied. "As I've mentioned before, blue energy itself can't harm humans. But raw monster magic bouncing freely around a sports park can do unbelievable mischief."

"Like what?" asked Jinx.

Doc shook his head grimly. "I have no way of predicting. Every time I ask my supercomputer that question, its genius brain goes into overload."

"What's the worst that could happen?" Jinx pressed.

"The worst case? You could see humans growing fish tails, witches sprouting dragon wings, werewolves turning into hairless humans. You name it, it could happen."

Wulf gasped. "Dude! You mean, I could become...a bald human...forever?"

"Maybe not for *that* long," Doc replied. "But probably long enough to feel uncomfortable without your whiskers."

Bela gave a loud gulp. "Say, guys," he said. "I've just had a fabulous idea. How about if all of you go to the games alone this year and I sort of, stay home? That way I can make sure we get everything on videotape, from start to finish."

"Chill, Bela," Jinx scolded in a low voice. "This is no time for a bat to turn chicken."

"So what's our game plan for Halloween, Doc?" inquired Val.

"The tried and true one," Doc replied. "Today and tomorrow I want each of you to exercise and practice for your events. Then tomorrow night, I want all of you to get a good night's sleep. I need you to be in top physical and mental condition."

"What about our tubes of MPF 1313, Doc?" Steiner asked.

Doc slapped his forehead. "Thanks for reminding me. It had totally slipped my mind." He paused for a minute to think. "Damon knows by now that Val has the tubes. So we can't leave them here overnight. I'll need another one of you to take them away and find somewhere safe to store them until the games tomorrow."

"I'll do it, Doc," said Steiner, raising his hand. "I know a good hiding place a couple of blocks from our house."

"Excellent, son," Doc replied. "I'll also need you to fetch the tubes for me tomorrow so that I can check them one last time before the games. Then you can take them along with you to the sports park."

"Gotcha!" Steiner replied.

"In the meantime," Doc went on, "I'm going to crank out more formula. We probably won't have enough tubes to protect everyone at the games," he said. "But we may be able to protect a couple hundred monsters. The big challenge, of course, will be to persuade them to put it on. Like T. Rex, they may think we're just trying to pull off some ridiculous Halloween hoax."

Doc put on his knapsack and headed out of the

garage. Before hopping into his L.U.V., he turned and said, "Let's hope for the best, but be prepared for the worst. Ready or not, Howl-O-Ween Games here we come!"

At 9:00 p.m. sharp on Halloween, T. Rexford Snattly waddled out into a grassy field in the center of the BMX dirt track at the Monsterey Valley Extreme Sports Park. After making a brief welcoming speech, the League president, who was dressed as a kazoo, gave a quick hand signal.

"Let the Howl-O-Ween Games begin!" T. Rex shouted into a microphone.

Suddenly a hundred spotlights flashed on. Night turned into day. Slowly the satellite dishes surrounding the park lifted their silver faces toward the rising moon. A giant television screen on top of the scoreboard lit up. And a huge roar went up from the crowd of spectators, dressed their coolest for the festivities. The most eagerly awaited sports event in Monsterey Valley was finally under way.

The Extreme Monsters' captain was not in a happy mood, though. Outfitted as a kid-sized grandfather clock, Val was growing increasingly anxious with every tick of his costume. The half-mile BMX race was set to start in 25 minutes. Steiner was the team's star entry in the event, but he hadn't arrived yet. Even more troubling, Doc hadn't shown up either.

The last time Val had spoken to him was about two hours ago. Doc had reported that he was almost finished making the last batch of MPF. All he had to do was to fill the tubes with lotion. Once that was done, he intended to drive directly over to the sports park and meet the Extreme Monsters. Val hadn't heard a word from Doc since then, and the scientist wasn't answering his home phone, his cell phone, or his pager. That was not a good sign.

Val knew it wasn't like Steiner or Doc to be late for a competition, especially one as important as this. Not only did Val need them to field a full team, but he also needed their tubes of moonscreen. Most monsters at the sports park already had on their regular-strength moonblocker. Some wore it in the form of colorful body paint. Without any MPF to shield them, the Extreme Monsters were at the mercy of the rising moon.

Val stared at the moon as it hung, seemingly motionless, above the stadium. It was large and round, a bright, ghostly white. There wasn't a trace of blue in it—or even a hint of blueness yet to come. But whether the moon was colored blue or white didn't matter much to Val at that moment. It was a full moon, and already Val could feel his forehead beginning to tingle. It was the first sign one of his bad lunar headaches was coming on. He knew that Wulf and Jinx and Mumford were probably feeling it, too. Unless Steiner or Doc arrived soon with the MPF, Val wasn't sure the Extreme Monsters could safely participate in any events. That would give a giant boost to Team Pendant's chances of sweeping the games.

Then he heard it—a rhythmic, metallic noise in the distance. It was approaching fast, extremely fast. Val sighed with relief. His super hearing was detecting the familiar and unmistakable pumping sound of Steiner on his BMX. Val unlatched the hinges of his clock costume, swung open the clock face, and peered in the direction of the sound. He could see Steiner now. He was zipping toward the sports park, up and down a roller coaster of soft brown hills.

Two minutes later, Steiner came to a screeching halt in front of Val, his wheels spitting rocks and dirt. He was dressed as a shining knight, complete

with aluminum-foil armor and a silverized plastic helmet with a red plume.

"Where have you been?" Val asked. "Your race starts in 20 minutes."

Steiner yanked off his helmet. He was gasping for air. "Got...tubes...for...Doc...to...check...like... we...agreed.   While...I...was...out...of...house... Damon's...goons...ambushed...Doc.   They... jumped...me...when...I...returned. I...broke...loose. Doc...kidnapped."

Val's face paled. *"Kidnapped?* Doc? Oh, no! And the MPF?"

"All stolen...except...for these." He handed Val a torn paper bag containing three MPF 1313 tubes. "This is...all...I could grab back."

Val took the bag and stuffed it inside the door of his clock. "Did you recognize any of the goons?"

"Just Clem and Cletus Sline for sure," Steiner panted. "I saw them stuff Doc into one of Damon's communications vans. I saw the number before they drove off—" Steiner hung his head in shame. "I failed, Val," he muttered. "I failed Doc and I failed the team."

"Wrong!" responded Val. "You did the best you could. You kept Damon from getting all the MPF. You found out where they're hiding Doc. And you got away yourself." He looked Steiner in the eyes, and said, "Be honest with me. Are you able to ride?"

"Absolutely. Cletus Sline is riding against me in the half-mile BMX. I'm not going to let him get away with what he did. I'm going to make him eat dirt."

"That's our Steiner!" exclaimed Val, giving him a high-five. Val quickly examined Steiner's bike for signs of damage. It looked fit to ride. Then he handed Steiner a Neutralizer Wristband. "Hurry, there are only 16 minutes left," he said. "Put on this wristband and ditch your armor. There's no rule you have to wear a costume *during* a race. We've got to get some MPF 1313 on you."

Steiner shook his head. "I don't want any."

"Don't be crazy."

"I'm not. We only have three tubes for five athletes. My costume's shiny. It reflects light. Maybe it will protect me from the full moon. Use the tubes for yourself and the others."

"It's too dangerous," Val said. "It might work while the moon's still white. But what will happen when the moon turns blue? I don't want to risk it."

"Sorry, captain," Steiner said, flipping down his visor. "I'm not giving you a choice." And with that, he shot off on his bike toward the BMX starting line, leaving Val holding the bag.

PUZZLE 6

Directions:

Use the clues below to find the correct answers in the word hunt. (Be careful! The words may read from right to left or from down to up.) Then shade in the letters with a pencil. The shaded letters form a letter of the alphabet.

The name of Doc's blue-moonscreen formula: _ _ _ _ _ _ _ .

Wulf fears he might be turned him into "a _ _ _ _ human."

Val goes to the Howl-O-Ween Games in a grandfather _ _ _ _ _ costume.

Steiner rides to the Howl-O-Ween Games dressed as a shining _ _ _ _ _ _.

Find the words:

D	E	R	E	T	A	V	E	R	Z	9	C
L	L	B	M	X	A	T	O	A	S	L	H
N	I	A	S	B	1	Q	U	X	O	S	I
F	3	K	B	T	A	A	P	C	Y	E	T
R	F	V	2	3	L	P	K	V	3	1	A
E	B	E	L	A	1	K		A	F	D	B
4	O	A	E	B	N	3	9	L	B	O	I
N	R	B	W	I	R	E	1	G	B	C	3
3	J	M	G	W	6	P	W	F	1	K	1
M	C	H	E	M	O	O	N	1	P	S	3
P	T	W	E	R	E	W	O	L	F	M	1
C	X	N	B	U	H	O	W	L	O	W	F

Write the letter in the secret code box provided on page 91.

CHAPTER SEVEN

The Blue-Moon Effect

Val was standing trackside with Jinx, Wulf, and Mumford, who had hurried over to the stadium to catch Steiner's race. The four made an odd-looking group. Next to Val in his grandfather clock outfit was Wulf, dressed as a Swiss accordion salesman. Jinx was decked out as the Golden Gate Bridge. Of all the Extreme Monsters, Mumford had put the least effort into his costume. All he'd done, it seemed, was wind hundreds of yards of wool around his mummy wrappings. When Jinx had quizzed him about what he was supposed to be, Mumford had mumbled, "a ball of yarn."

As the Extreme Monsters awaited the start of Steiner's event, Val briefed them on Doc's kidnapping and the theft of the MPF 1313. It was all he could do to keep Wulf from jumping over the guardrail—accordion and all—and going after Cletus.

"We'll deal with him later," Val said. "Right now we have some races to win, and some people and monsters to protect. That's what Doc would want us to do."

"I agree," said Jinx. "Besides, I don't think Damon would dare harm Doc. All he probably wants to do is keep him out of action for the games."

"Or force him to reveal the secret of his new formula," growled Wulf, still fuming.

"I have an idea," Jinx said. "Mumford's speed-climbing events aren't scheduled until way later."

"Right. So?" said Val.

"So while we're competing, he could snoop around the park, looking for Doc and the missing moonscreen. Once he finds them, we can figure out a way to get them back."

"Works for me," Val said.

"Me, too," said Wulf.

"How about you, Mumford?" inquired Val. "Are you up for it?"

Mumford nodded yes.

"Excellent," Val replied.

The public address system crackled on. "Attention, attention!" a voice boomed out. "BMX racers, take your places!"

"Here, everyone," Val said. "Put on some MPF." He opened up the paper bag Steiner had given him and passed out the tubes. Much to his surprise, Mumford, like Steiner, refused to take one. Mumford said magical bandages were enough to block lunar rays. With the full moon getting brighter and his headache getting worse,

Val had neither the time nor the patience to argue with a mummy. So as Mumford wandered off on his scouting mission, Val squeezed out a whole tube of MPF 1313 and applied it to his skin. Almost instantly, his headache stopped. Doc's formula worked like a charm!

At last, Val felt free to turn his attention back to the games. Steiner's event was a half-mile race—twice around the quarter-mile track—with the fastest finisher winning. The BMX course was laid out in a squiggly loop, like a lasso dropped on the ground. It had tight corners and tricky jumps over steep dirt mounds and watery moats.

The bikers were lined up at the starting line. Their leg muscles tensed for the push-off. Val could see that each of them was wearing a Neutralizer Wristband. That meant Cletus couldn't use any of his magical powers to "accidentally" squirt skidding slime under Steiner's wheels, or thermal or gluey slime into his gears. So far, so good.

The official at the starting line raised his electronic pistol. "Get ready...get set ..."

BLAMMM!!!

The field of eight BMX bikers exploded off the line in a cloud of dust. Cletus shot into the lead, managing to box Steiner in behind four slower riders. On the first turn, the Slime Brother leaned way down and grabbed a handful of dirt and rocks. As he accelerated into the straightaway, he tossed the rocks over his shoulder so they'd rain down on his opponents. Hidden by the fog of churned dirt, Cletus's dirty trick went unnoticed by the judges.

Coming into the first jump, Cletus opened up a strong ten-yard lead. As he soared over the first hill, grabbing big air, he glanced back and grinned mockingly at Steiner. The Extreme Monster was wiping grit and dirt off his plastic visor. He was struggling to find a way to punch through the sluggish pack.

Steiner took the jump with a burst of speed. As he sailed over the crest, he decided to show the crowd that an Extreme Monster couldn't be pushed around. He pulled an electrifying 360, flipping his bike forward end over end until he landed upright, spewing dirt, on the crest of the next hill. It was an amazing jump of more than 80 feet. In one move, Steiner had leapfrogged over the heads of the four more-cautious bikers. He was now solidly in second place.

At the moat, Steiner trailed by three yards. By the end of the first lap, he was hugging Cletus's tail. As the first jump came round again, Steiner pulled even. Cletus poured on the heat, but Steiner stuck with him. Taking the jump together, they both went airborne. Cletus performed a tail whip, spinning the back part of his bike around like a top, seeking to knock Steiner off his BMX. But Steiner saw the trick coming. With a mighty tug, he pulled his BMX up and over his opponent's. Still climbing, Steiner pulled off two more rotations. Cletus

gawked at Steiner's 1080 flip. The crowd gasped. Steiner touched down lightly on one wheel on the far side of the next crest. It was awesome.

Unfortunately, the Slime Brother didn't land as well. Cletus' BMX, still spinning, clipped the near side of the hill. Cletus flew over the handlebars and into a muddy ditch. It was a fitting end for the Pendant goon: Slime in the slime! Steiner couldn't help grinning as he pedaled to an easy win in record time.

This was just the beginning of the Extreme Monsters' rout of Team Pendant that night. Jinx swept all her street-luge events. Wulf utterly destroyed Clem Sline in the half-pipe competition. Val set a new Howl-O-Ween record in street skateboarding. Then Steiner returned to nab another Gold in the BMX street-riding event. At the midnight break for entertainment, the scoreboard showed the Extreme Monsters in first place by an unbeatable margin. Team Pendant was third, due to a good showing by Scott Squire in the freestyle in-line event.

Just as the Numb Skulls were setting up on stage for their rock concert, a buzz went through the crowd. Fingers, paws, and claws pointed up toward the moon.

"Dudes, look!" Wulf cried out. "The moon's going *KA-BLUEY!*"

Sure enough, just as Doc had predicted, the full moon was turning bright blue. The earth darkened. The temperature dropped. And the air crackled with magic.

Val felt his stomach knotting up. "Uh-oh," he said under his breath, "I guess it's final show time in lunar land."

"Guys, check it out!" Jinx exclaimed, gesturing toward the stage. The Numb Skulls were a group of extremely unusual musical zombies. But at the moment they looked more extremely unusual than usual. The lead singer was trying to stuff a chair into his ear. The lead guitarist was mooing into his boots. The bassist's head had sprouted a unicorn horn.

Val scanned the audience. Dozens of monster athletes were scattered among the crowd. Each was wearing a Neutralizer Wristband. Val could see that all the wristbands were glowing. Some were giving off huge sparks. That could mean only one thing—the Neutralizer circuits were overloading. Raw monster energy was pouring into the air. Wild, crazy magic was on the loose and effecting everyone monsters and humans too.

Next to Val, a centaur dressed as a lost sock suddenly morphed into a pair of dice. A teenage yeti on a skateboard *poofed* into a creature that was half crow, half book bag. Two humans munching on hot dogs calmly decided to switch heads. A girl who'd come as an exclamation mark screamed when she saw that she'd grown vampire fangs and a mermaid's fin.

Bolts of monster energy were shooting from wristbands everywhere. They bounced off objects and zapped whoever was in the way. With each new zap came a shocking change in shape and personality.

Jinx checked her watch. "Omigosh!" she cried, stepping carefully over a cyclops who'd shrunk to the size of a chipmunk. "There are 12 minutes and 40 seconds more of this!"

Val heard a deep whirring noise. Damon's satellite dishes had switched to full power. The eight collection dishes were now focused on the moon. They were greedily soaking up oodles and oodles of blue-moon rays.

Val felt a tug at the back of his clock suit.

"I found him," said a small voice.

Val turned around. "Mum-Man! That's terrific! You found Doc?"

The little mummy nodded. He motioned for Val to follow him.

"Hey, guys!" Val called to his teammates. "We're going to rescue Doc!"

Mumford led the Extreme Monsters to a large satellite van. It was covered with a huge plastic sheet painted to look like branches and leaves.

"Camouflage," whispered Val as a bolt of magic smashed into a nearby tree. "This is probably Damon's control center."

Mumford lifted up a flap in the back. Above the license plate was stenciled the number "37." Val noticed a thick red cable running from the dish atop the van to a giant storage battery a few yards away. Smaller black cables branched out from the large red one. Val guessed they had to be the feeder cables from Damon's other dishes.

Val ran over and felt the sides of the battery.

"Uh-oh!" he said.

"What?" Jinx asked.

"It's swelling."

"The battery's swelling?" said Jinx.

"Swelling and trembling."

"Swelling and trembling?" repeated Wulf.

"Swelling and trembling and hot."

"Uh-oh!" said Jinx.

While they were talking, the battery had started to bulge way out. It began trembling so violently it made the ground shake.

Val had an idea. "Steiner! Shake the van!" As Steiner gripped the side of the van and used his great strength to rock the vehicle back and forth, Val cupped his hands to his lips and yelled, "Earthquake! Earthquake! Run for your lives!"

An instant later, the door to the van flew open. A terrified Damon stumbled out, falling on his face. "What's happened to me?" he cried, as he discovered his new look: lizard skin and a pig snout.

Cletus and Clem hopped out after him. They'd been changed into a pair of identical tonsils. Having no feet, they slipped on their own slime and piled up on top of their boss.

Last to emerge was Vincent. The raven tried to flee

through a window. A bolt of magic hit him first, though, and turned him into a mosquito bite.

While Val dashed inside the van to free Doc, Mumford unwound some of his yarn and used it to tie up Damon and his henchmen. Val found Doc sitting in a chair strumming on a guitar. A bolt of magic had changed him into Elvis.

"Drop the strings, Doc," Val shouted. "We've got to shut down the battery."

"Ah can't stop playin'," drawled the musical Doc.

"Then tell *me* what to do!" Val pleaded.

"Flip switch five!" Doc sang. "That'll reverse the poles."

Val flipped the switch. Almost immediately the ground stopped shaking. Val looked out the window. The storage battery was de-bulging. Blue-moon rays were shooting harmlessly up into space. The pressure was off. And disaster had been avoided.

Val heard Jinx giving the countdown. "Four seconds...three seconds...two...one ...."

Val and a finger-picking Elvis ran outside. They looked up. The moon was no longer blue. They looked around. No sparking wristbands. Monsters and people were rubbing their eyes as if they'd just awakened from a very bad dream. One by one they were *poofing* back to their old selves. With relief, Val heard the Numb Skulls tuning up for their first number. When he turned to congratulate Elvis, he found Doc standing beside him instead. Even Damon and his gang looked normal again.

Doc was grinning from ear to ear. "We did it, Val! We foiled Damon's plan. And we all made it through the blue moon alive."

"And don't forget—we also won team gold," Wulf added. "Team Pendant choked."

Doc had Mumford untie Damon and the Slime Brothers.

"Grrr," said Damon, picking himself up off the ground. "You may have won this round, Extreme Monsters. But you won't win the next one."

Jinx snapped her fingers and her magic wand appeared before her. "Hey, guys," she said. "Wanna see what Damon looks like with a mouse's head?"

"You wouldn't," said Damon, starting to back away. "Would you?"

"Gobbling Turkey, Moldy Bread..." chanted Jinx, waving her wand menacingly.

Without waiting to hear the rest, Damon and his henchmen turned tail and ran. Val burst out laughing. So did Jinx and Doc and all the other Monsters.

Doc gave a weary smile. "Extreme Monsters," he said. "Just thank your lucky stars that a blue moon only comes...well...once in a blue moon!"

Directions:

Below is a substitution code. Each letter or symbol in the code stands for a single letter of the alphabet or a punctuation mark. For example, the word **"dog"** would be written as **"#;<"** in this code. Your secret code should now be complete!

LETTER CODE KEY

a	b	c	d	e	f	g	h	i	j	k	l	m	n
%	G	@	#	J	$	<	F	^	X	5	L	Q	P

o	p	q	r	s	t	u	v	w	x	y	z	,	'	.
;	B	A	E	7	8	W	?	R	>	H	C	Y	/	K

SECRET MESSAGE TO DECODE

<	;	G	G	L	^	P	<		8	W	E	5	J	H	Y
Q	;	L	#	H		G	E	%	#	Y					
<	^	?	J		;	L	#		#	%	Q	;	P		
%		Q	;	W	7	J	/	7		F	J	%	#	K	

A.
Melting ice cubes,
On the lawn,
Fried bananas
Make me yawn.

B.
Gobbling turkey,
Moldy Bread,
Give Old Damon
A Mouse's head.

C.
Gobbling turkey,
Moldy Bread,
Wish Old Damon
Stayed in bed.

Write the letter of the correct answer in the secret code box provided on page 91.

BE SURE TO VISIT THE OFFICIAL WEBSITE OF THE

EXTREME MONSTERS™

AT WWW.EXTREMEMONSTERS.COM

- FIND OUT ABOUT NEW EXTREME MONSTERS BOOKS AND GEAR
- READ CHARACTER BIOS
- PLAY EXCLUSIVE GAMES
- DISCOVER MORE ABOUT MONSTEREY
- LEARN ACTION SPORTS TERMS, TIPS, AND TRICKS
- READ THE QUOTE OF THE DAY AND MUCH, MUCH MORE!

VISIT EXTREMEMONSTERS.COM TODAY!
IT'S SPOOK-TACULAR!

SECRET CODE

Directions:

Write your answers in the space under the puzzle number.

CODE KEY

Puzzle No.	1	2A	2B	2C	2D	3	4	5	6	7
Answer										

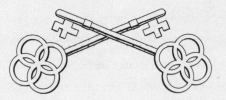

And now visit

www.extrememonsters.com

and type in the secret code in the code key above.

You'll unlock extra games and features.

Plus, you'll learn more about the Extreme Monsters and their thrilling world!

If you need help with any of the puzzles, an answer key can be found on the website too!

GLOSSARY

Aerial *(skating, skateboard, BMX)* Any trick done in the air.

Berani *(skating)* A front flip with a 180 in it.

Flame *(street luge)* Urethane luge wheels actually catching fire as a result of high speed.

Grind *(skating, skateboarding, BMX)* Sliding along an edge using your trucks, pegs, or the side of your skates.

Kickflip *(skateboard)* In a kickflip, the skater kicks the board with the ball of his or her front foot, the skateboard flips and spins over at least once, and the skateboarder lands on the board comfortably, wheels down, and rides away.

Ollie *(skateboard)* A skateboarding trick where the skateboarder pops the skateboard into the air. The effect is the skateboarder jumping with the skateboard stuck to his or her feet.

Paddle Zone *(street luge)* Area between the starting line and the beginning of the road course where pilots use their hands to develop downhill momentum.

Skitching *(skateboard, skating)* Being towed by a rope (or bandage) from a bicycle.

Sled *(street luge)* Another term for the luge.

Spew (a wheel) *(street luge)* To blow a wheel off your luge

Tailwhip *(BMX)* Trick performed on the ground or in the air involving the back end of the bike rotating completely around as the front end remains straight.

Trucks *(skateboard)* The metal T-shaped part that mounts onto the underside of the skateboard

Urethane *(skating/skateboarding/street luge)* Rubber-like substance that skate wheels are made of.

360 *(skating, skateboarding, BMX)* Spinning completely around (360 degrees) so you end up facing the same direction you started facing.

50/50 Grind *(skateboard)* A 50-50 grind is when a skateboarder grinds with both trucks. When most skaters grind something, they use both trucks, and so are 50-50ing whatever they are grinding on.

1080 *(BMX)* Three complete rotations in the air, probably the most spins possible on a BMX bike